To my husband, for showing me the world, and to my traveling children, who see it with us.

www.mascotbooks.com

The Traveling Children: Journey Through Italy

For more information, please contact:
Mascot Books
620 Herndon Parkway #320
Herndon, VA 20170
info@mascotbooks.com

Library of Congress Control Number: 2018911251

CPSIA Code: PRT0519A
ISBN-13: 978-1-68401-954-0

Printed in the United States

The Traveling Children

JOURNEY THROUGH Italy

Scarlett
Hayes

illustrated by
Ariel Friesner

In the middle of London, there was a house with a green door. Inside this house lived a boy named Hayden and his little sister, Avery. Hayden and Avery lived with their parents and their dog, Max. One day, while Hayden and Avery were playing pirates (their favorite game), they overheard their parents talking in their bedroom.

"The children will love it there," they heard Mum say. "I can't wait for them to ride a Vespa."

"We'll have to keep a close eye on them, though. They are very curious children, and they tend to wander off. It's easy to get lost in a big city," they heard Dad say.

Mum agreed. "They could sneak off to follow the smell of fresh pizza, and who knows where they'd end up!"

A big city with Vespas and fresh pizza? Hayden and Avery could not contain their excitement any longer. They burst into their parent's room.

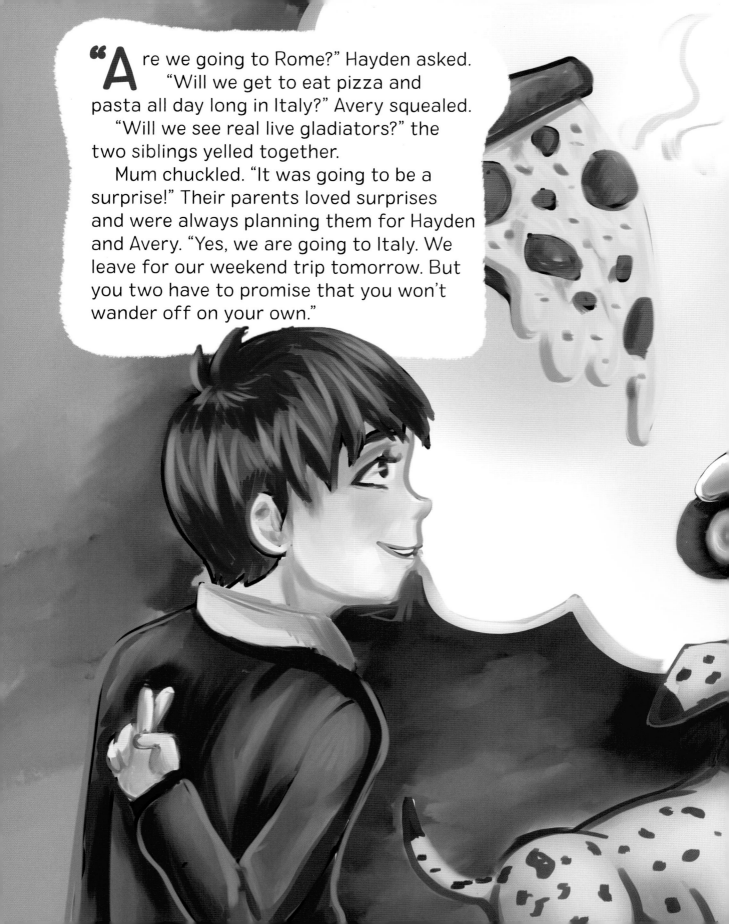

"Are we going to Rome?" Hayden asked. "Will we get to eat pizza and pasta all day long in Italy?" Avery squealed.

"Will we see real live gladiators?" the two siblings yelled together.

Mum chuckled. "It was going to be a surprise!" Their parents loved surprises and were always planning them for Hayden and Avery. "Yes, we are going to Italy. We leave for our weekend trip tomorrow. But you two have to promise that you won't wander off on your own."

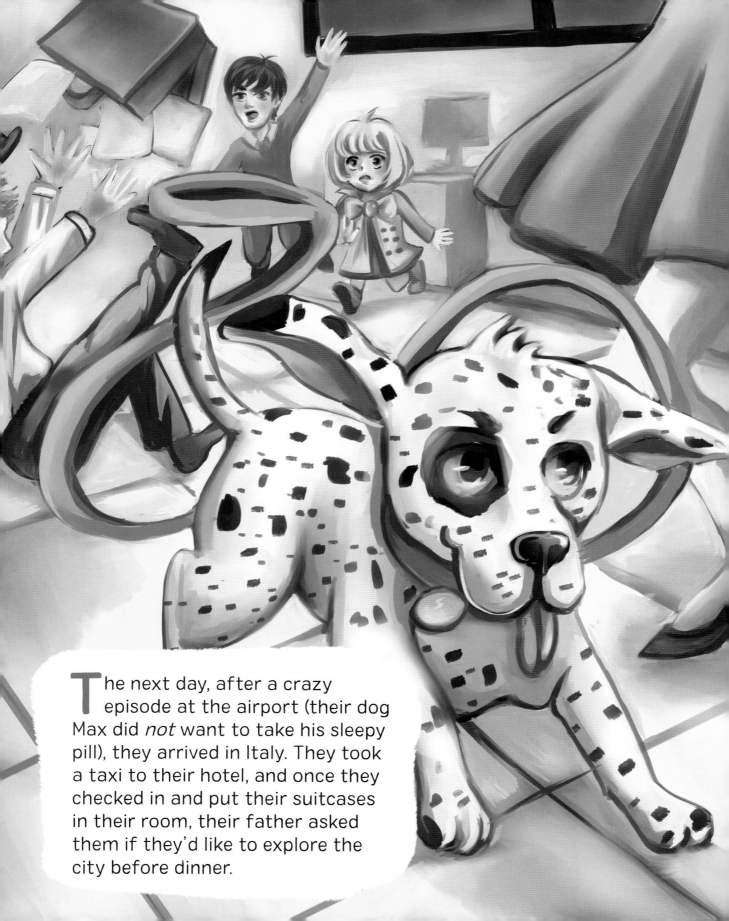

The next day, after a crazy episode at the airport (their dog Max did *not* want to take his sleepy pill), they arrived in Italy. They took a taxi to their hotel, and once they checked in and put their suitcases in their room, their father asked them if they'd like to explore the city before dinner.

"Italy is a magical place, but it is also a very busy city. You must stay with us at all times," their father said.

"Of course!"

"Great! Let's head to the Colosseum."

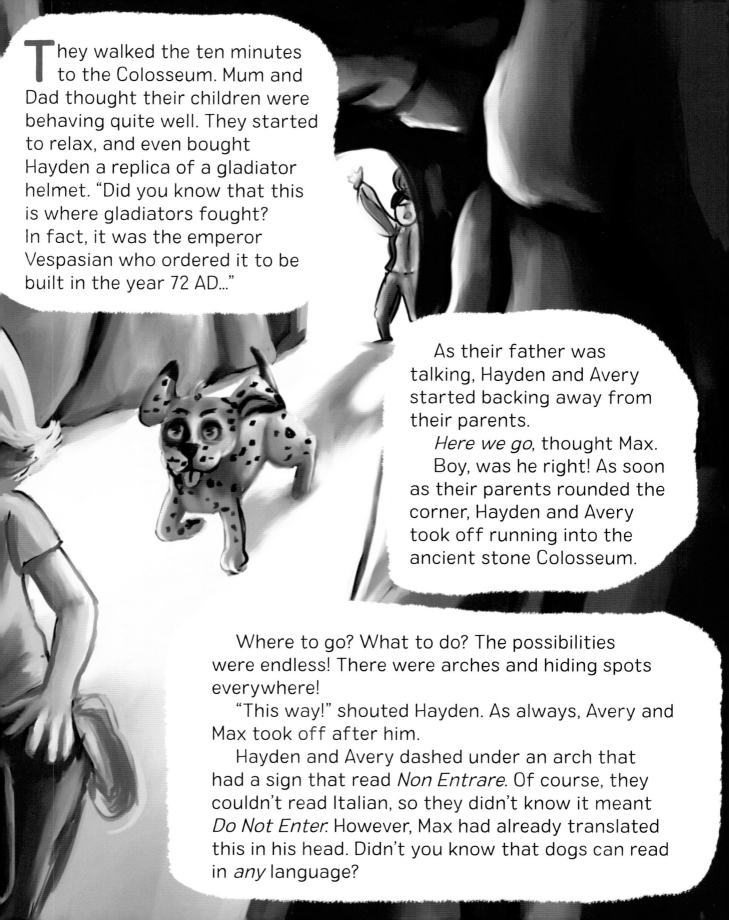

They walked the ten minutes to the Colosseum. Mum and Dad thought their children were behaving quite well. They started to relax, and even bought Hayden a replica of a gladiator helmet. "Did you know that this is where gladiators fought? In fact, it was the emperor Vespasian who ordered it to be built in the year 72 AD..."

As their father was talking, Hayden and Avery started backing away from their parents.

Here we go, thought Max.

Boy, was he right! As soon as their parents rounded the corner, Hayden and Avery took off running into the ancient stone Colosseum.

Where to go? What to do? The possibilities were endless! There were arches and hiding spots everywhere!

"This way!" shouted Hayden. As always, Avery and Max took off after him.

Hayden and Avery dashed under an arch that had a sign that read *Non Entrare*. Of course, they couldn't read Italian, so they didn't know it meant *Do Not Enter*. However, Max had already translated this in his head. Didn't you know that dogs can read in *any* language?

own through the tunnels they ran until Avery slammed into a very large cage. "Ow!" Avery called out. She then heard a loud roar. The cage spun, and a mysterious foggy light clouded the room. It passed in seconds, but Avery and Hayden felt like ages had passed by the time it lifted. As her eyes adjusted to the dark, she saw a large Bengal tiger in the cage.

Two guards dressed in funny clothes entered the tunnels. "I've found the Royal Highnesses!" one yelled. "We've been looking for you everywhere. Let's go you two, we can't start the battles without you!" The tall guard escorted them up a secret pathway until they came to a balcony. Several people were already there, and they all immediately bowed when they saw Hayden and Avery. At the front of the balcony were two chairs with little crowns made of leaves on them.

"Your seats, your Royal Highnesses," said the guard, who gave a low bow.

Although Hayden and Avery had no idea what was going on, they put the leaves on top of their heads and sat in the chairs. Hayden clapped his hands and yelled "Let the games begin!" He was a natural.

Immediately, gladiators came out from the left side while the tigers were released from the right side. Hayden and Avery watched in amazement while the ancient gladiators and the glorious tigers fought. The tiger from the tunnels let out another earthshaking roar.

"Hayden! Avery! Max!" they heard someone yell. Hayden turned around.

"We are royalty! You will call us...Oh! Hi, Mum!"

They saw the angry faces of their parents. "We were just watching the gladiators fight the tigers..." but when he turned to look where he was pointing, there was nothing there but a pile of old stones. On his head, he wasn't wearing anything except for a bunch of twigs.

"Let's go. We have been looking everywhere for you guys!" yelled their parents.

When they left, they didn't get back into a taxi. Instead, they saw two scooters waiting for them. "This is how a lot of people in Italy travel. Vespas!" their dad said excitedly. Hayden and Max jumped on the back with their dad, while Avery climbed on with their mum. Off they went down the cobblestone streets.

The next day, their parents announced that they were all going to church. "Church? It's not Sunday, and I thought we were on vacation!" said Hayden.

"Italy is a very religious country. You can't come here and not see the Vatican!" exclaimed their mum.

An hour later, they arrived at the Vatican. "This is Vatican City," she said. "It's actually its own country, and the smallest one in the world!"

Vatican City looked like a semi-circle surrounded by sculptures. In the middle was a ginormous, tall, pointy stone with a little cross on the top. "They say that parts of the cross that Jesus died on are inside that little cross," explained their father. "Some of the most famous artists of all time helped create this city, like Michelangelo and Leonardo."

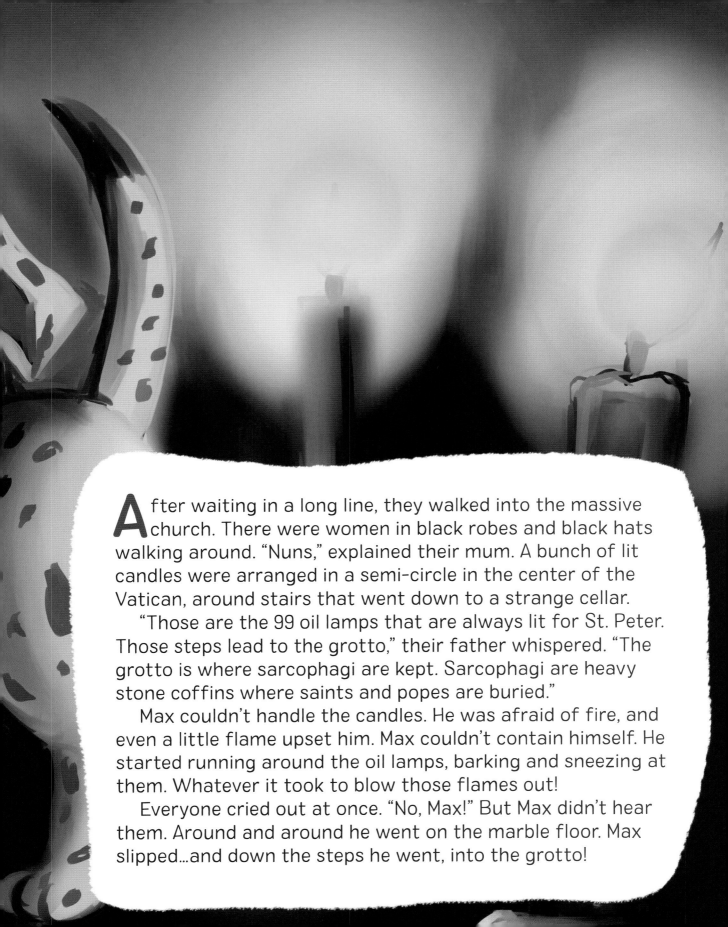

After waiting in a long line, they walked into the massive church. There were women in black robes and black hats walking around. "Nuns," explained their mum. A bunch of lit candles were arranged in a semi-circle in the center of the Vatican, around stairs that went down to a strange cellar.

"Those are the 99 oil lamps that are always lit for St. Peter. Those steps lead to the grotto," their father whispered. "The grotto is where sarcophagi are kept. Sarcophagi are heavy stone coffins where saints and popes are buried."

Max couldn't handle the candles. He was afraid of fire, and even a little flame upset him. Max couldn't contain himself. He started running around the oil lamps, barking and sneezing at them. Whatever it took to blow those flames out!

Everyone cried out at once. "No, Max!" But Max didn't hear them. Around and around he went on the marble floor. Max slipped...and down the steps he went, into the grotto!

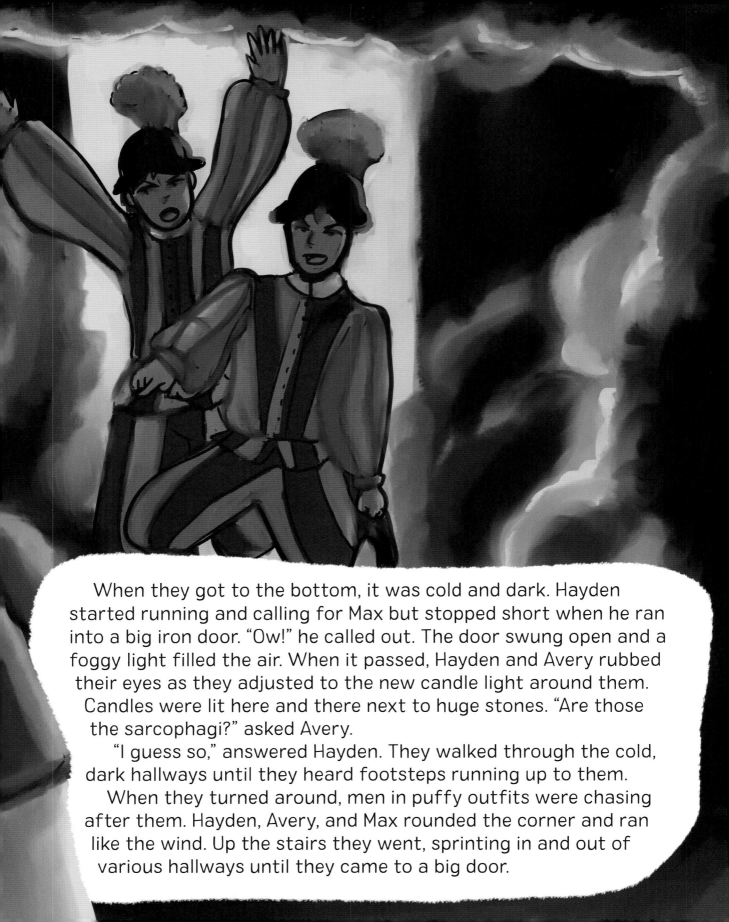

When they got to the bottom, it was cold and dark. Hayden started running and calling for Max but stopped short when he ran into a big iron door. "Ow!" he called out. The door swung open and a foggy light filled the air. When it passed, Hayden and Avery rubbed their eyes as they adjusted to the new candle light around them. Candles were lit here and there next to huge stones. "Are those the sarcophagi?" asked Avery.

"I guess so," answered Hayden. They walked through the cold, dark hallways until they heard footsteps running up to them.

When they turned around, men in puffy outfits were chasing after them. Hayden, Avery, and Max rounded the corner and ran like the wind. Up the stairs they went, sprinting in and out of various hallways until they came to a big door.

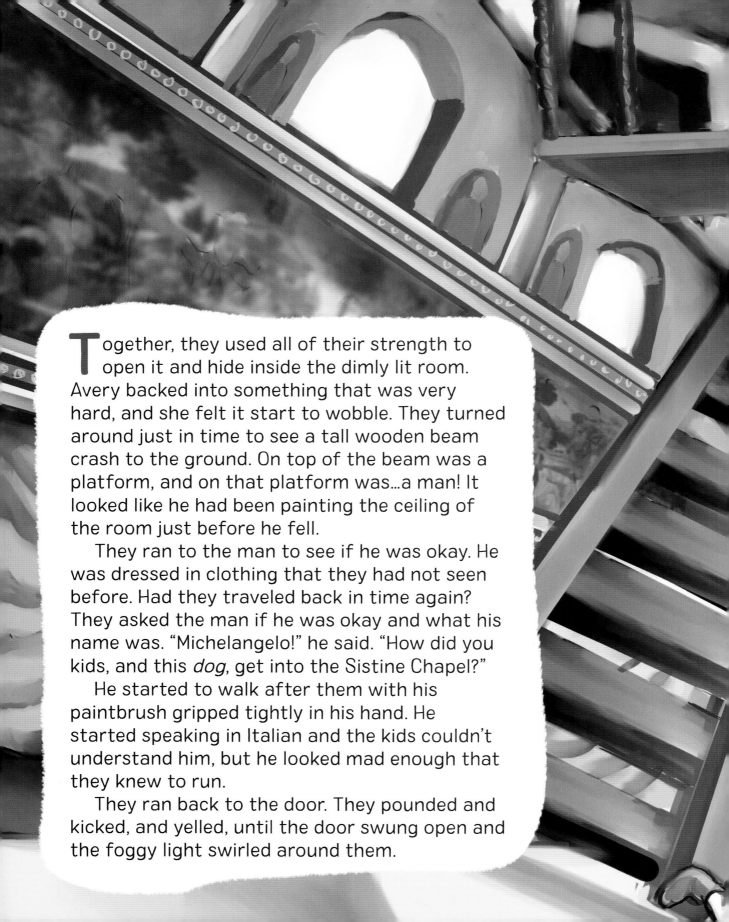

Together, they used all of their strength to open it and hide inside the dimly lit room. Avery backed into something that was very hard, and she felt it start to wobble. They turned around just in time to see a tall wooden beam crash to the ground. On top of the beam was a platform, and on that platform was…a man! It looked like he had been painting the ceiling of the room just before he fell.

They ran to the man to see if he was okay. He was dressed in clothing that they had not seen before. Had they traveled back in time again? They asked the man if he was okay and what his name was. "Michelangelo!" he said. "How did you kids, and this *dog*, get into the Sistine Chapel?"

He started to walk after them with his paintbrush gripped tightly in his hand. He started speaking in Italian and the kids couldn't understand him, but he looked mad enough that they knew to run.

They ran back to the door. They pounded and kicked, and yelled, until the door swung open and the foggy light swirled around them.

Avery and Hayden toppled out into sunlight. When they reached the outside they heard someone yell, "Hop on!"
It was their parents on the Vespas!
They raced through the city and back to their villa.

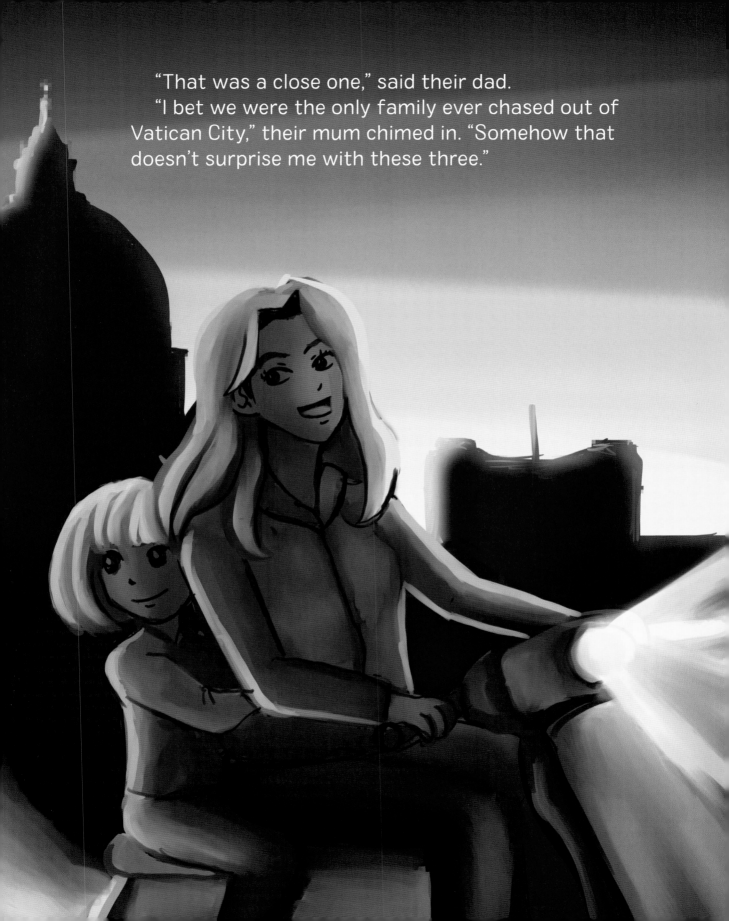

"That was a close one," said their dad.

"I bet we were the only family ever chased out of Vatican City," their mum chimed in. "Somehow that doesn't surprise me with these three."

When the weekend was over and the family was back in London, Hayden and Avery overheard their parents talking. "Next summer, Aunt Lilly wants to visit us in London. I wonder if we should bring the children to show her around. After all, they're always getting into trouble."

Hayden and Avery looked at each other from their beds in their shared room and smiled as they listened to their parents talk about their next adventure.

About the Author

Scarlett Hayes is a mother and teacher. When she isn't working with students, she enjoys writing and traveling with her family, which includes her husband and three children. This is her first children's book.